This book contains sexual content, mostly expressed through genitalia-laden landscapes and provocative wording. I have written the following with humor and from the perspective of a bisexual, cisgender woman because that is what I know, not because I believe it is the only form of sexual expression or identification. I understand the intricacies of the vulva and vagina, and the importance of using the correct language when making a distinction between the two, however, for the sake of rhyming and gusto, I have chosen to primarily use 'pussy.' Plus, it's time we reclaim and reframe that word. Pussies are powerful! Any use of girl/lady/woman or pronouns she/her are meant to be inclusionary and serve as one chosen identifier within a broad spectrum, including trans and gender-non-conforming. I have used "you" where applicable, as the primary guide. For those who haven't enjoyed orgasms or sexual pleasure, it's my hope that this light-hearted book opens up a world of possibility and discussion. Sexual autonomy and fulfillment are imperative for equality. Let us come together.

Second Edition — 2020

theorgasmbook.com
@theorgasmbook

Find the author:
@NicolleDoubleL
@GirlsWhoSayFuck

Oh, the places you'll go oh oh! / by Nicolle Hodges
illustrated by Jillian Mundy

Summary:
Sexual empowerment for women in rhyme form. A meandering tale through the potential highs and lows of discovering oneself, from Sexual Debut to owning pleasure, overcoming shame, and realizing the life-changing power of orgasms.

ISBN: 978-1-7771250-3-5

Published by
GWSF Creative

Oh, the Places You'll Go Oh Oh!

By Nicolle Hodges

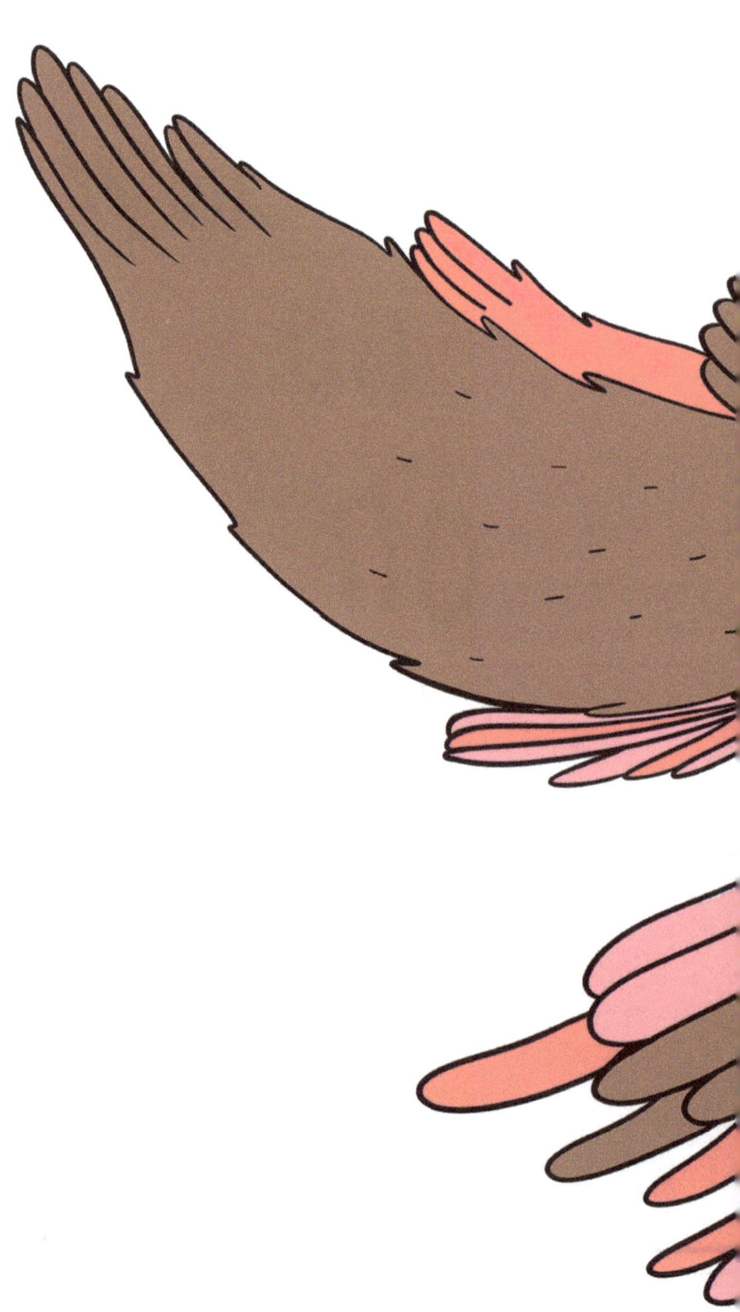

illustrated by
Jillian Mundy

Huzzah, hurray!
You did it today.
You burst through the bubble,
Get off on your way!

You have stuff in your pants.
You have things that you know.
You have guesses and questions
and things you can show.

Set out from this spot, ‘cause you’ve got the key.
Unlock all the boxes. It’s you that you’ll please!

If pleasure comes slowly
then that's okay too.
The world is your stage.
It's your Sexual Debut!
Cum This Way

What's happening down there?
Don't worry. Don't stress.
Just have a good look!
You should know yours the best.

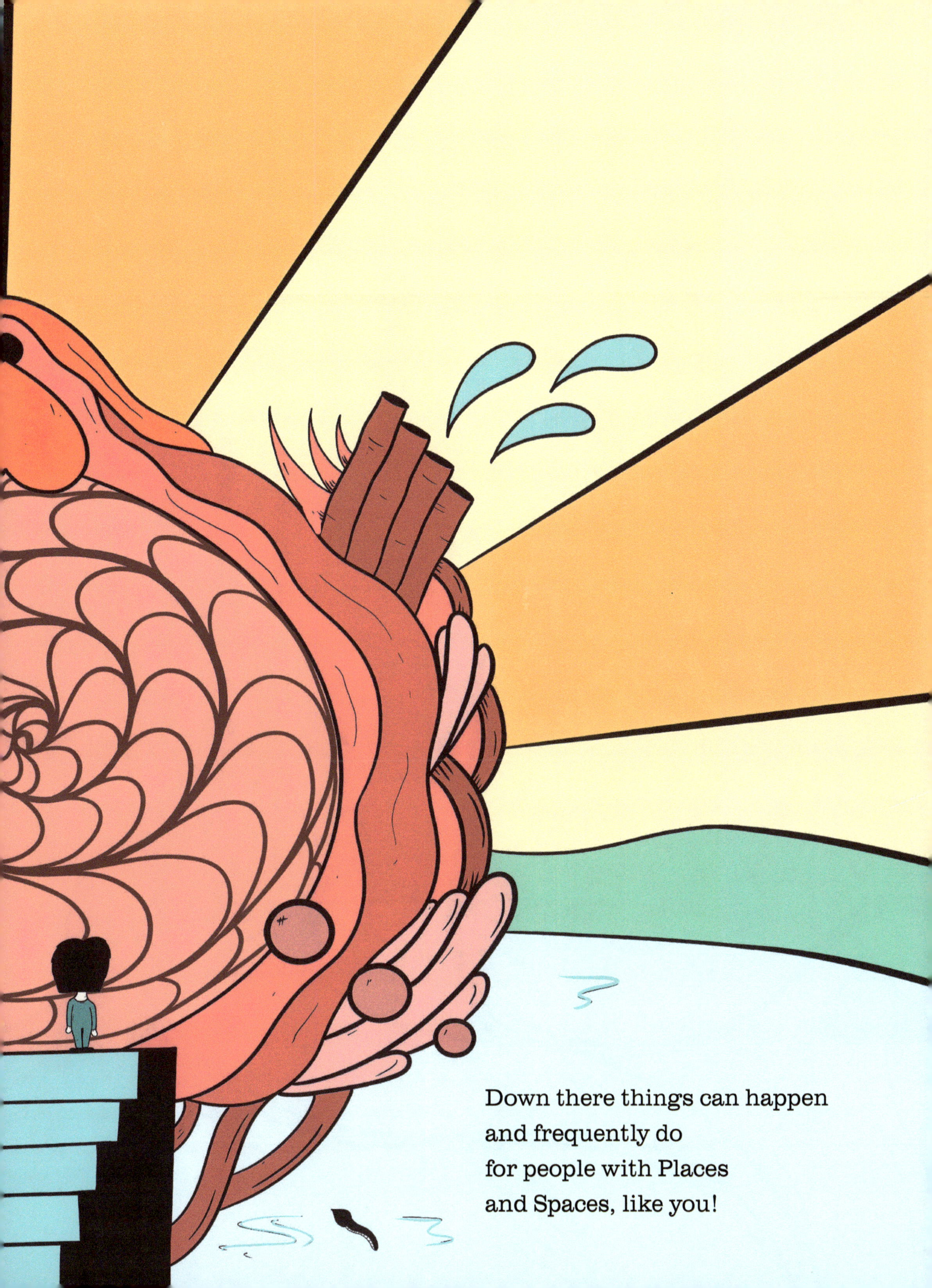

Down there things can happen
and frequently do
for people with Places
and Spaces, like you!

You'll get to discover the ways that you come
and learn all about where your pleasure comes from.
You'll try what you wish. Why not try something new?
They're simply amazing, the things you can do!

Oh,
THE PLACES
YOU'LL GO
oh oh!

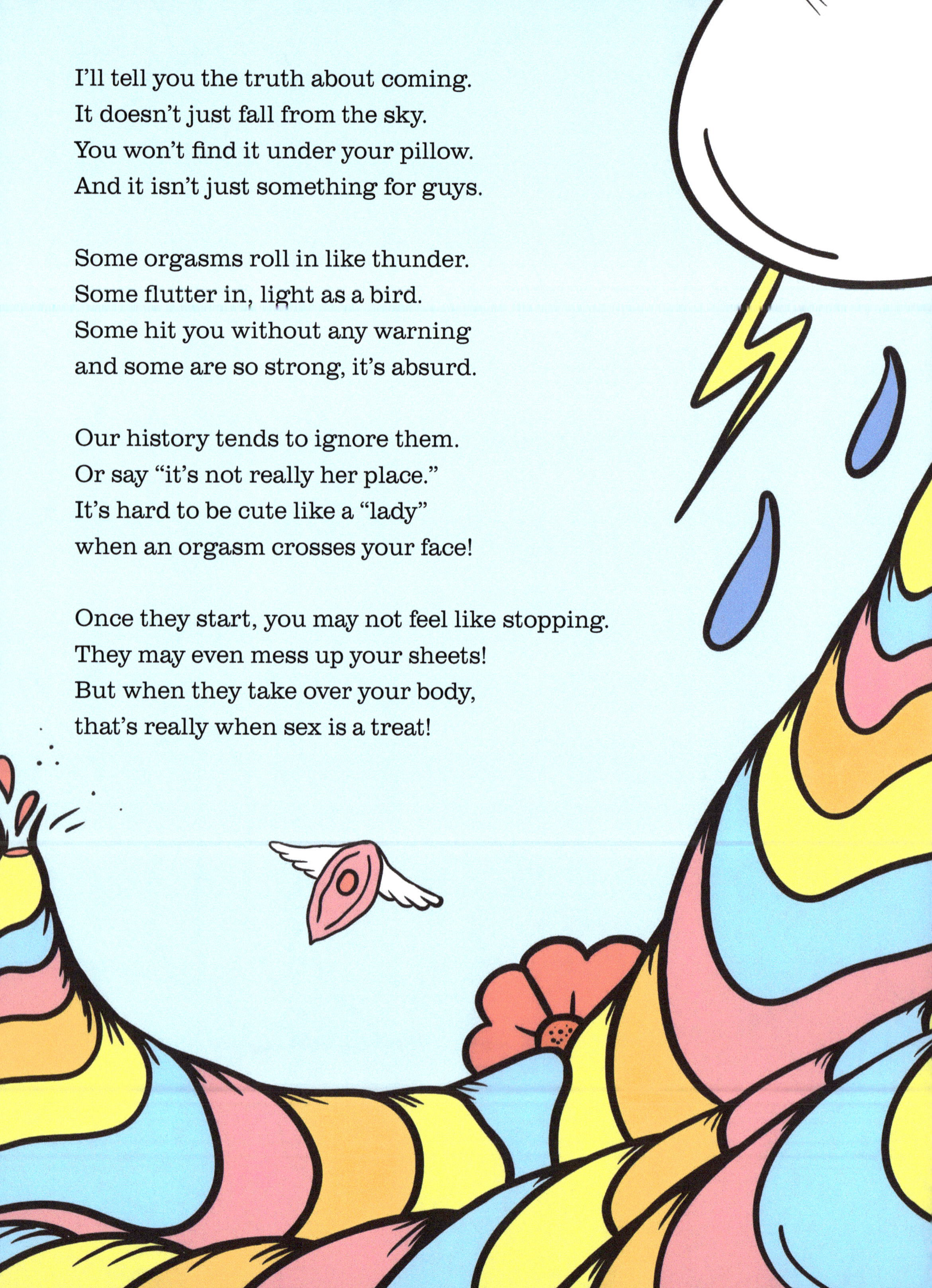

I'll tell you the truth about coming.
It doesn't just fall from the sky.
You won't find it under your pillow.
And it isn't just something for guys.

Some orgasms roll in like thunder.
Some flutter in, light as a bird.
Some hit you without any warning
and some are so strong, it's absurd.

Our history tends to ignore them.
Or say "it's not really her place."
It's hard to be cute like a "lady"
when an orgasm crosses your face!

Once they start, you may not feel like stopping.
They may even mess up your sheets!
But when they take over your body,
that's really when sex is a treat!

Getting to places takes patience.
Our bodies evolve and they change!
But one thing is true about pleasure,
it's better the less you feel shame.

Once you have harnessed your power,
you'll see that it's scary for some.
You'll keep going and going and going.
They'll have to hold on while you come!

Sometimes you will win and you'll be on a roll!
You'll pass snortles and scoffers and Snarky Van Snolls.
And no shaming or taming will stifle your strumming,
it's the greatest adventure to simply be-coming!

Except sometimes it isn't.
It's sad but it's true.
Sometimes, you get Nowhere
and feel Nothing too.

You'll find potholes and loopholes and cuckolds galore!
Pterodicktyles and scribbles like "whore" on a door.

YOU UP?

Things that slobber and foam, that feast, squawk and dingle.
Texts from your exes, but not when you're single.

Build-ups and hang-ups and breakups and hiccups,
hookups and makeups, and calls that are wake-ups.

The cocktothorpes, though, are the worst of the bunch!
They stare at you like you're their breakfast AND lunch.

Oh! Those cocktothorpes squabble to get you to bed.
They squawk and they talk with the worst of their heads.

And though heads of a thorpe squawk as much as they do,
they don't have much to say once the squawking is through.

You may get confused
and want to be done!
So you and your vulva set out on a run.
Where are you running? There's no time to choose,
and you're headed, I fear, to a place of abuse.

The Shaming Place...

....full of people just shaming.
Shaming for the clothes you wear
or how you grow your body hair.
Shaming what's between your legs,
saying you'll run out of eggs.
Shaming all the things you've tried,
ignoring all your reasons why.
Shaming what they see as "sin"
for all the lovers you've let in.
Shaming what you think is hot.
Everyone is shaming! And they shame quite a lot.

Shaming 'cause they're scared of sex.
Shaming 'cause they hate their ex.
Shaming 'cause they can't admit
that on your face they'd like to sit.
Shaming's what their parents did
but you don't have to take it, kid!

NO!
Shame's not for you!

And shaming yourself isn't something you'll do!

Soon you'll get out
and get back on your way!
You'll find stranger places
where strangers can play.
And playing's more fun when you find others who
can say what they want, so that you say it too.

oh oh oh!

FREAK

With clits a clip-clapping
once more you will reign!
On this vulva crusade
you will soon stake your claim.
Those going your way
won't settle for lame.
When you say "Oh My God!"
you're just saying your name!

As you start to let go of that silly old shame,
you may find some pleasure in feeling some pain.
Spanking as thanking, restraint as release,
being tied up, or wearing a leash.

Those are some things which we're sadly not taught.
But those who enjoy them, enjoy them a lot!

They're out there to find,
all your freaky new friends.
And once you have met them, the fun never ends.
There's whipping, and smacking, and tying up knots.
And going to places you thought you could not.

Oh, the places you'll go oh oh!

There is much to be touched! There are things to explore.
There is sex with yourself. Or with two. Maybe more!

And the magical thing about doing what's true,
it makes you the you-iest you'er of you!
The world wants to know how you do what you do!

Queen! You'll be queenly as queenly can be,
with your pussy empowered, you'll soon take the lead!

You set out to be-come
and Oh! Places you went.
Some days you felt straight
and on some you felt bent.

You went many places
and on you'll be going.
Your pleasure a river
that keeps overflowing.

You'll keep right on learning.
You'll grow and you'll grow.
You'll even go places
that nobody knows.

You'll light up the sky
and shoot up to the moon!
You'll own your own body,
it's more than a womb!

Remember this...

The universe is between your legs.
You are the creator of all things!
Your pleasure is a source of power,
and orgasms can give you wings.

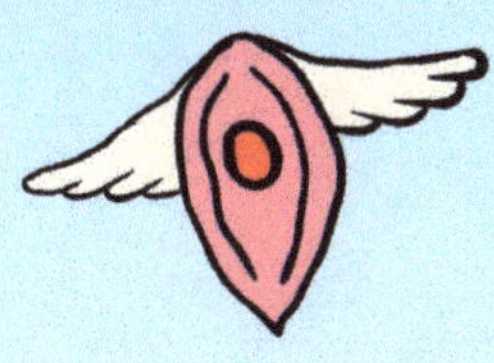

Thank your Pussy!

Be you Lulu or Charlie or Jacob or June,
born with a pussy or getting one soon,
get off to your Places!
Your pleasure awaits!
It's never the end.
And it's never too late.

The answer is in you.
You are the key!
Find out for yourself.
Don't take it from me!

This book would not have been possible without the support and encouragement from the following people. Words cannot express my gratitude. This is for you:

Christopher Weatherstone, Rachel Colic, Madeline Zysk, Matthew Ehrenreich, Taylor Oakes, Tyler and Connor Fyfe, Mika Unterman, Steph Payne, Jonah Brotman, Dan McCann, Tonya Surman, Kate Whelan, David Purcell, Monica Polo, Clinton Robinson, Scott Biggart, Robin Banister, Emily Thring, Cait Brenchley, Fatimah Gilani, Dan Sutton, Corey Herscu, Parul Bansal, Jeremie Saunders and Bryde MacLean, Nikolas Badminton, Dessy Pavlova, Mark Hauk, Nicolas Pateras, Cindy Tran, Mike Reid, Peter Harvey, Ben Koppel, Joshua Seinen, Jer Baum, Joanie Martineau, Luciano Foschi, Summer Dhillon, Bradley Gretzinger, Jessica Brown, Alyson Strike, Lisa Harun, Kathleen Robinson, Daniel and Charlaine Robinson, Kieley Beaudry, Rachael Modrcin, Marisa Hunter, Mauricio Alanis, Oz Zandiyeh, Dieter and Danielle Macpherson, Brandon Wright, Paul Crowe, Emily Leung, Tara Teng, Jan Werthwein, Brandon Sousa, R.K. Gandhi, Sarah-Jane Nelson, Orane Cheung, Andres Markwart, Devawn Blackwood, Aasttha Khajuria, Vicki Duong, Calandra Balfour, Michael Drexler, Stacie Hunter, Ashleigh Brown, Alexis Tataryn, Larkyn Statten, Kylie Spring, Kristen Franklin, Calla Lee, Claire Oakley, Jeremy Gosse, Matthew Belanger, Cory Lewis, Olivia Wallis, Tina Chapman, Jordan Specht, Daniel Motyka, Miroslav Tomoski, Rory Friedman; and my parents: Paul Hodges, Petra Niemeyer, Greg Bowie. Finally, Jonas Caruana: With you, I was able to reach into that special place and pull back this book. Thank you.

All of my love goes to these brilliant humans for their insane talents and strange brains. You brought this book from nothingness to somethingness:

Illustrator: Jillian Mundy @snake.tiddy

Designer: Sierra Holmes @sierras_designs / @sierra_holmes_

Advisory board:

Dr. Stephen de Wit DHS, MPH, ACS
Sexologist - Speaker - Coach
drdewit.com

Kaitlyn Goldsmith, Ph.D., Registered Psychologist
Instructor - University of British Columbia - Vancouver Campus
Clinical Health Psychologist - Women's Clinic
- Vancouver General Hospital
kaitlyngoldsmith.com

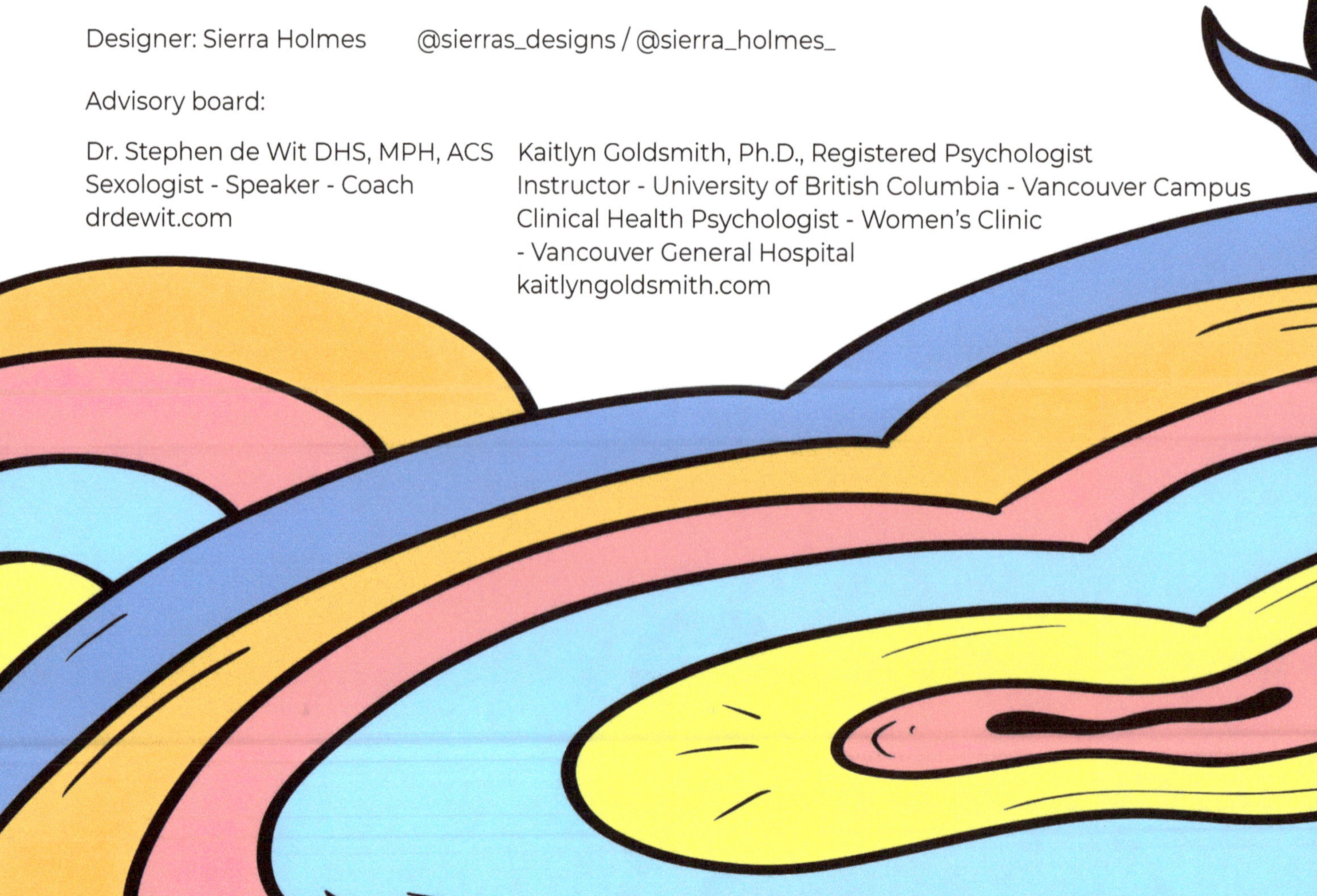

www.ingramcontent.com/pod-product-compliance
Lightning Source LLC
Chambersburg PA
CBHW041154300726
48981CB00003B/249
9781777125035